Book Club Edition

**Walt Disney Productions
presents**

Donald at the
Seashore

Random House 🏠 New York

Donald Duck is taking Daisy and his nephews to the beach today.

"Oh, boy!" say Huey, Dewey, and Louie when they see the water.

Off they go for a swim.

Donald and Daisy unpack the car.

umbrella

Here are some things
that the ducks brought
to the beach.

towels

picnic basket

ball

fins

snorkel and mask

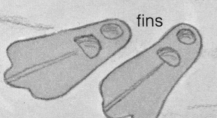

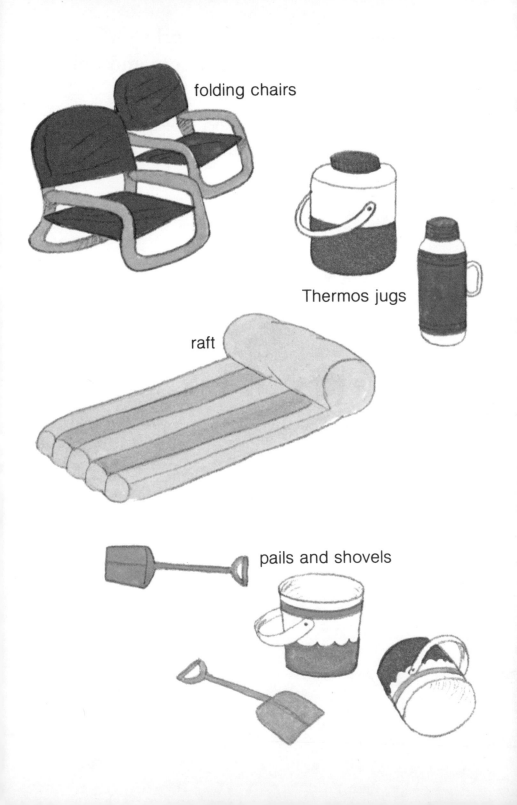

folding chairs

Thermos jugs

raft

pails and shovels

Dewey is ready to go snorkeling.

He wants to see the plants and animals that live in the ocean.

The snorkel tube lets him breathe while his face is in the water.

Huey likes to lie on the raft.

He bobs up and down on the waves.

The hot sun beats down on him and makes him sleepy.

Be careful, Huey! Don't get sunburned!

The lifeguard watches
everyone in the water.

Louie is building a fancy sand castle
in the damp sand near the water's edge.

Along comes
a big wave...

and that's the end of THAT sand castle!

"Time for lunch, boys!" calls Donald.

"Just one more swim!" say the boys,
and they dive back in the water.

Lunch tastes extra good at the beach.
Nobody minds when a little sand gets
in the food.

After lunch Donald and the boys fly kites.
There is always a breeze at the seashore.

It's still too soon after lunch to go swimming.

"I'm going for a walk," says Donald.

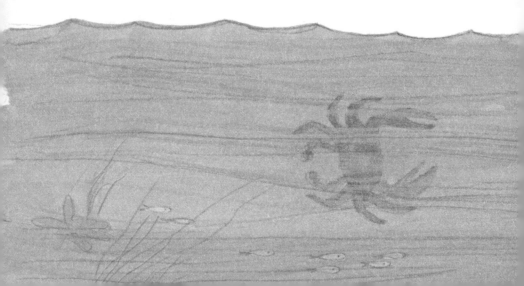

Daisy decides to stay under the umbrella and read her book.

Donald sees a crab
in the water.
"I wonder if I can
catch it in my net,"
he says.

YEE-OW-W! The crab
catches Donald instead!
It gives Donald's toe
a big pinch.

Huey, Dewey, and Louie are taking
a walk too.

"Guess what we saw, Uncle Donald!"
calls Louie.

Here are some things that Donald's nephews saw in the shallow water along the shore.

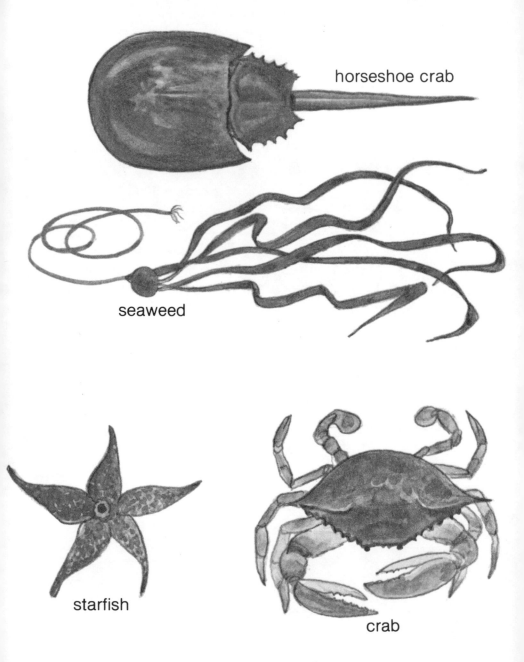

horseshoe crab

seaweed

starfish

crab

seashells

clam

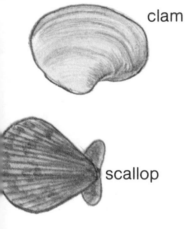

mussel

scallop

flounder

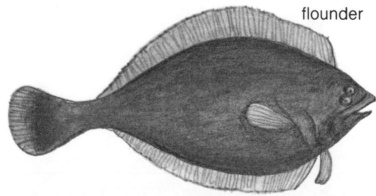

On the way back Donald and the boys
see many shore birds.

Gulls fly overhead.

Sandpipers run along the water's edge,
looking for things to eat.

After one more swim, it's time
to go home.
Everyone helps pack the car.

"Thank you, Uncle Donald," say the boys as they leave the beach.

What a wonderful day it has been!